WHAT THE LITTLE PIG SAW

What the little pig saw,

When he went round the world,

Caused his ears to stick up,

And his tail to be curled.

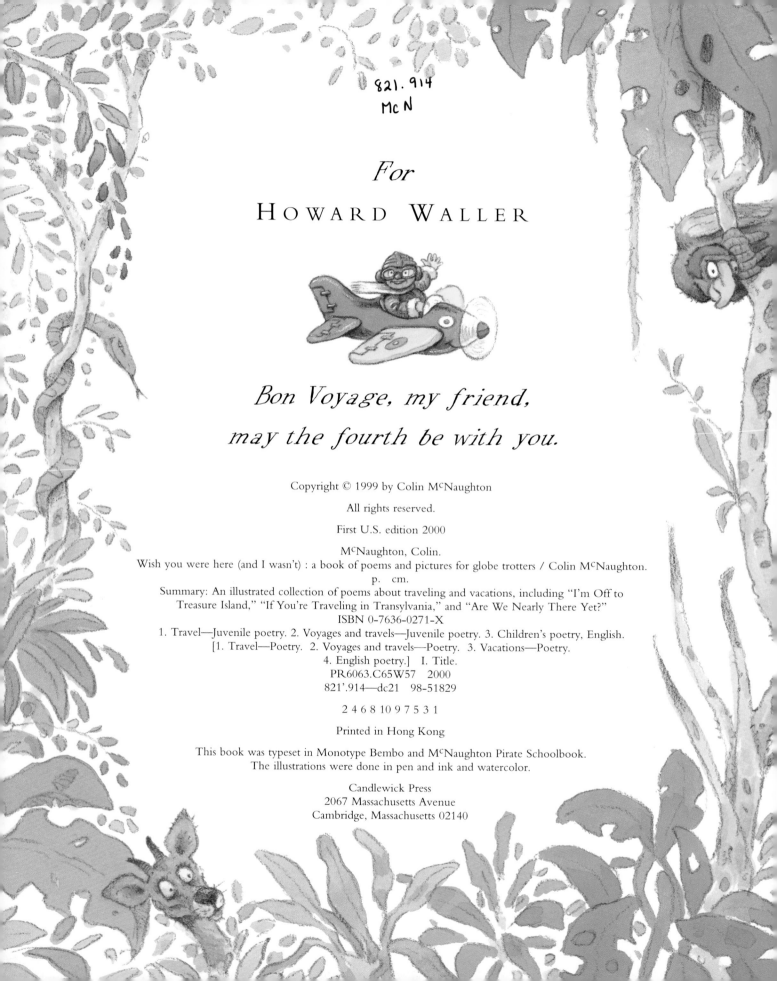

For

HOWARD WALLER

Bon Voyage, my friend,
may the fourth be with you.

First U.S. edition 2000

McNaughton, Colin.
Wish you were here (and I wasn't) : a book of poems and pictures for globe trotters / Colin McNaughton.
p.   cm.
Summary: An illustrated collection of poems about traveling and vacations, including "I'm Off to Treasure Island," "If You're Traveling in Transylvania," and "Are We Nearly There Yet?"
ISBN 0-7636-0271-X
1. Travel—Juvenile poetry. 2. Voyages and travels—Juvenile poetry. 3. Children's poetry, English.
[1. Travel—Poetry. 2. Voyages and travels—Poetry. 3. Vacations—Poetry.
4. English poetry.]   I. Title.
PR6063.C65W57   2000
821'.914—dc21   98-51829

2 4 6 8 10 9 7 5 3 1

Printed in Hong Kong

This book was typeset in Monotype Bembo and McNaughton Pirate Schoolbook.
The illustrations were done in pen and ink and watercolor.

Candlewick Press
2067 Massachusetts Avenue
Cambridge, Massachusetts 02140

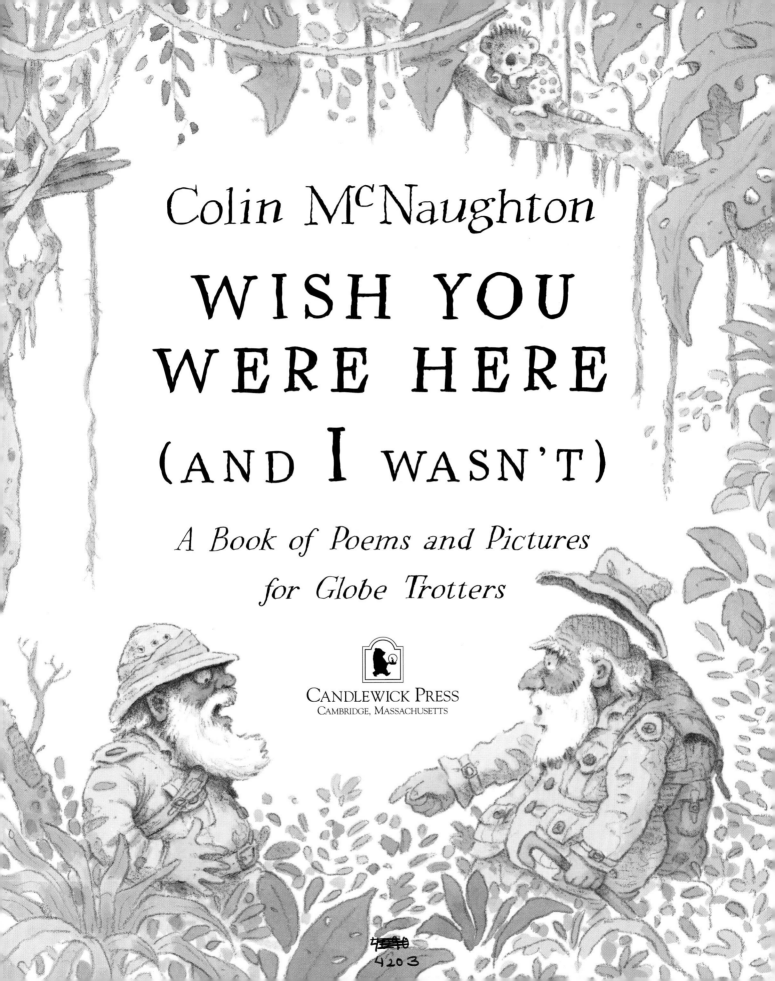

Colin McNaughton

WISH YOU WERE HERE

(AND I WASN'T)

A Book of Poems and Pictures

for Globe Trotters

CANDLEWICK PRESS
CAMBRIDGE, MASSACHUSETTS

WISH YOU WERE HERE

Dear All,

The sea looks great, but I've not tested—

    Locals say it's shark-infested.

Beach looks fine, I'm not complaining—

    Go there, soon as it stops raining.

The food's okay, if you like fish—

    And things that crawl across your dish.

As for our hotel, it's neat—

    It should be great when it's complete.

I'll bring you back a souvenir—

    Good-bye for now, wish you were here.

        (And I wasn't!)

THE OOZILY WOOZILY PLONK

There's the Hairily Scarily Donk,
And the Heavily Devily Conk.
    But none is as weird
    Or so horribly feared
As the Oozily Woozily Plonk.

He likes nothing more than a chat,
But I'd strongly advise against that!
    Just get on your bike
    Because you wouldn't like
What the Plonk means by "chewing the fat."

It is awfully bad manners, I know,
But just make your excuses and go.
    No, don't even smile,
    Run a four-minute mile
If a Plonk says so much as "Hello!"

Should a Plonk ever hunt you and find you,
He'd certainly crush you and grind you.
    But there's nothing to fear,
    There are none around here . . .

GOOD HEAVENS, THERE'S ONE

RIGHT BEHIND YOU!!!!!!!!!!!!!!!!

I'M OFF TO TREASURE ISLAND

The first verse is the chorus and can be repeated
after every verse—depending on how silly you're feeling.

Ooh-aargh, avast, ha-har!
  Ooh-aargh, avast, ha-har!
I'm off to Treasure Island,
  Ooh-aargh, avast, ha-har!

Most folks go to Blackpool,
  To Spain or Turkey, but
I'm off to Treasure Island—
  I'm a Treasure Island nut!

I'll sail the *Hispaniola*,
  A cutlass at my side;
I'm off to Treasure Island
  On the early morning tide.

I'll curse an' spit, me hearties!
  I'll tame the wildest sea!
I'm off to Treasure Island—
  It's a pirate's life for me!

I'll fly the Jolly Roger,
  Better stay out of me way!
I'm off to Treasure Island,
  I'll be gone by break of day!

"Pieces of eight!" cries Captain Flint.
  "There is no pirate bolder!"
I'm off to Treasure Island—
  With a parrot on me shoulder.

I'll follow Billy Bones's map,
  Meet up with old Ben Gunn.
I'm off to Treasure Island—
  Gonna have some pirate fun!

I'll sail home with me treasure,
   As rich as rich can be.
I'm off to Treasure Island—
   Do you want to come with me?

Yo-ho-ho an' a bottle of rum,
   Treasure Island here I come!
Long John Silver'd better run—
   I'm off to Treasure Island!

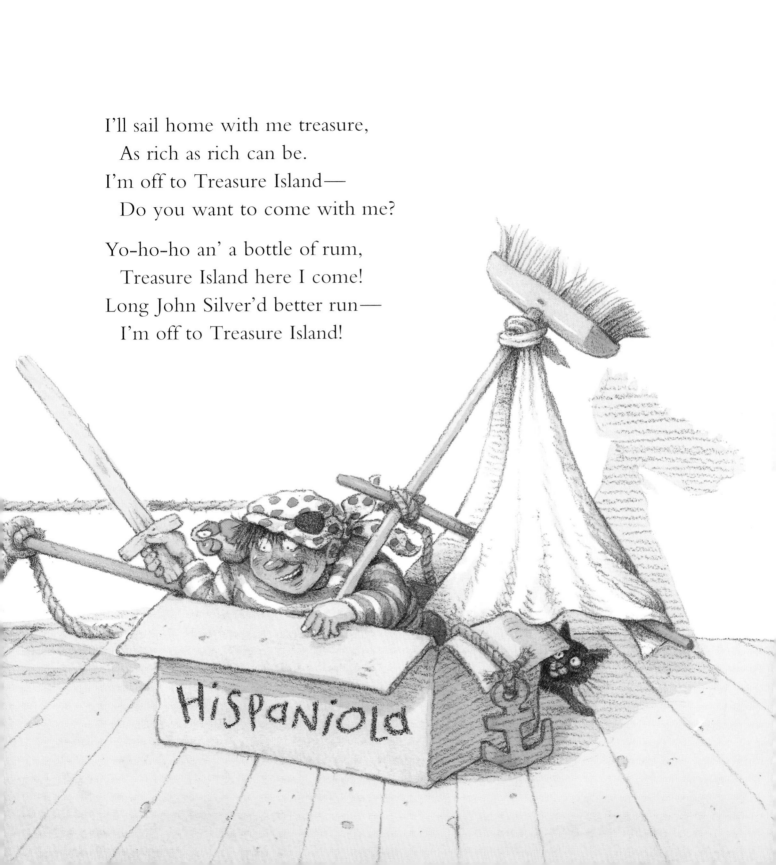

YET ANOTHER POEM TO SEND TO YOUR WORST ENEMY

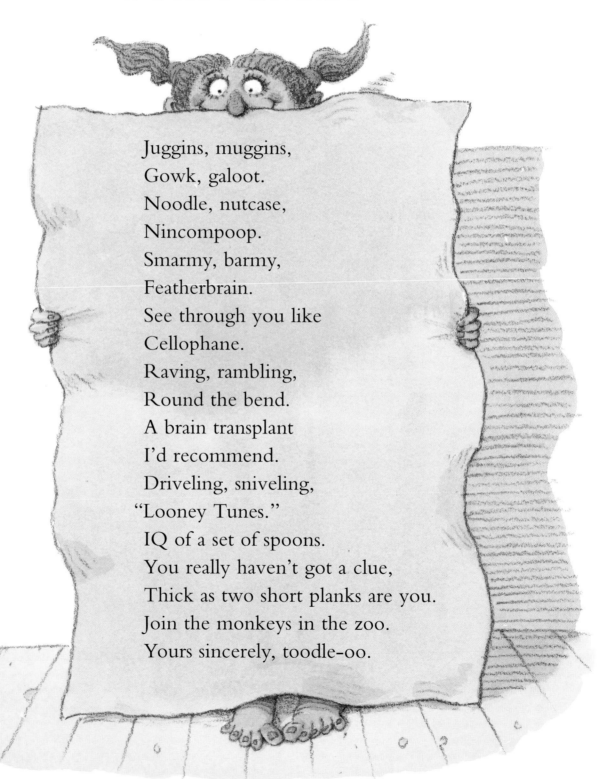

Juggins, muggins,
Gowk, galoot.
Noodle, nutcase,
Nincompoop.
Smarmy, barmy,
Featherbrain.
See through you like
Cellophane.
Raving, rambling,
Round the bend.
A brain transplant
I'd recommend.
Driveling, sniveling,
"Looney Tunes."
IQ of a set of spoons.
You really haven't got a clue,
Thick as two short planks are you.
Join the monkeys in the zoo.
Yours sincerely, toodle-oo.

THE ARMCHAIR TRAVELER

The armchair traveler drifts away
And takes a path he's often trod.
He gently strolls through fields of dreams,
A rambler in the Land of Nod.

THE POSTCARD

It's not that
I've got nothing
to write home
about—
it's just that
this place is
nothing to write
home about.

The Folks
Backhome
Ourtown

THE NOMAD RUSH

If in the desert you should be
And men on camels you should see
Going slowly, that would be
The famous Nomad Rush.

Through the desert dunes they ramble,
Drag their feet and sort of shamble,
Never rise above an amble.
That's the Nomad Rush.

They gaze into the clear blue sky
And half asleep they mosey by.
Now and then they'll maybe sigh.
That's the Nomad Rush.

They take their time, go nice 'n' easy.
Ooze on by, so cool and breezy.
Easy—peasy—lemon-squeezy—
That's the Nomad Rush.

IF I COULD FLY LIKE ICARUS

If I could fly like Icarus,
I'd really have some fun.
I'd pack a little suitcase
And fly off to the sun.

I'd fly so high I'd kiss the sky,
The clouds would be my bed.
I'd swoop so low, I'd call your name
And plop upon your head!

I'd fly around the world and back,
Yes, life would be a hoot.
I wouldn't change a thing, except—
I'd pack a parachute!

A STING IN THE TAIL

Two explorers, one called Splong
    (The other's name is Snit),
Meet by chance on a jungle path
    And chew the fat a bit.

Says Splong to Snit, "Please help me, do,
    For something puzzles me.
I've just seen something very strange
    Descending from a tree.

The body's pink, has purple stripes,
    With orange spots beneath.
The head is large; the mouth is huge,
    With great big pointy teeth.

From head to toe, this thing has spines,
    And legs, I counted nine.
It partly slithers, partly crawls,
    And leaves a trail of slime.

I've traveled this world over,
    Seen all there is to see,
But I've never seen the likes of this.
    I think you will agree."

"Pull the other one," says Snit.
    "I don't believe a word!
It's quite the most preposterous thing
    That I have ever heard!

There's no such insect, bird, or beast.
    You take me for a fool?"
But Splong, he does not take offense,
    Just smiles and keeps his cool.

"So what do you call this mythical beast?"
    Skeptical Snit he snorts.
"I've no idea," says Splong,
    "But one just crawled
        up the leg of your shorts."

ALL I ASK IS A PERFECT DAY

All I ask
   Is a perfect day
On a perfect beach
   In a perfect bay

In the perfect shade
   Of a perfect tree
With a perfect view
   Of a perfect sea

With a perfect breeze
   And a perfect sky
Read a perfect book
   Swat a perfect fly

In a perfect pool
   Find a perfect shell
Eat a perfect peach
   With a perfect smell

Skim a perfect stone
   Dig a perfect hole
Catch a perfect wave
   Score a perfect goal

Make a perfect dive
   See a perfect fish
With a perfect tail
   Give a perfect swish

Then in this perfect world
   Meet a perfect friend
And bring this perfect day
   To a perfect end.

A SAD CASE

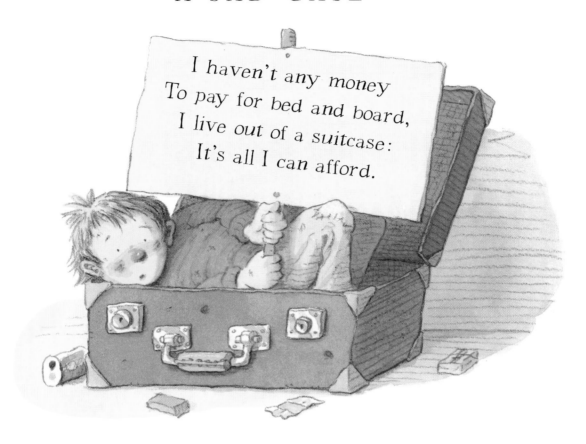

I haven't any money
To pay for bed and board,
I live out of a suitcase:
It's all I can afford.

ROW, ROW, ROW YOUR BATH

Row, row, row your bath,
Gently down the stream.
Pull the plug and watch your bath
Become a submarine.

Row, row, row your bath,
Smile and pull the plug.
Merrily, merrily, merrily, merrily,
Glug–glug–glug–glug–glug.

COUNTING ON YOU
(A Love Letter)

Love me WANDA,
   Love me TWODA,
Love me THREEDA,
   Love me FOURDA,
Love me FIVEDA,
   Love me SIXDA,
Love me SEVENDA,
   Love me EIGHTDA,
Love me NINEDA,
   Love me TENDA, do!

IF YOU'RE TRAVELING IN TRANSYLVANIA

If you're traveling in Transylvania
And you're all alone one night
And there's a terrible hammering on your door
And you wake with a terrible fright
And you open your door and standing there
Is a figure pale and green—
If he claims to be Count Dracula . . .
Just pray it's Halloween!

FIRST DRAFT OF THE MOST FAMOUS AUSTRALIAN SONG EVER

Once a jolly swagman
Camped by a billabong
Under the shade of a coolabah tree.
He unpacked his wallaby
And fired up his goolagong.
   "Who'll come a-waltzing with Hilda and me?

    Waltzing the builder,
    Waltzing St. Kilda,
      Who'll come a-waltzing with Hilda and me?"
      And he danced and he sang
      As he waited till his billy boiled.
        "Who'll come a-waltzing with Hilda and me?"

      And as that jolly swagman
      Waited till his billy boiled
       Under the shade of the coolabah tree—
       A man-eating crocodile
       Wearing nothing but a smile,
       Jumped from the billabong and bit him on the knee.

        Oh waltzing the builder . . . etc.

WELL, I HAVE!

Ever been lost in the Australian bush?
Ever been trekking in the Hindu Kush?
Ever gone skiing, got slush in the mush?
    Well, I have!

Ever got stuck on a mountainside?
Ever jumped a gap that was just too wide?
Ever got caught by an incoming tide?
    Well, I have!

Ever been sick on an aeroplane?
Ever been soaked by a monsoon rain?
Ever been caught in a hurricane?
    Well, I have!

Ever bounced across the sea in a hovercraft?
Ever sailed across a pond on a homemade raft?
Ever thrown a pebble down an old mine shaft?
    Well, I have!

Ever caught a catfish in the south of France?
Ever been swimming in your underpants?
Ever been bitten by giant ants?
    Well, I have!

Ever spent the day on a perfect beach?
Ever opened your shirt and discovered a leech?
Ever dived for a shell that was just out of reach?
  Well, I have!

Ever walked for hours in a rain forest gloom?
Ever found a cockroach in your hotel room?
Ever swum with stingrays in a blue lagoon?
  Well, I have!

Ever climbed a pyramid in Mexico?
Ever seen what you thought was a UFO?
Ever seen a shark from a pedalo?
  Well, I have!

Ever had a scorpion inside your shoe?
Ever pat the head of a kangaroo?
Ever take the hippy trail to Katmandu?
  Well, I have!

Ever run full speed down a giant dune?
Ever swum in the sea by the light of the moon?
Ever found that holidays end too soon?

WELL, I HAVE!

NO ROOM TO SWING A CAT!

My hotel room was tiny.
No room to swing a cat.
My cat was overjoyed and said
"Well, thank the Lord for that!"

FISHING FOR COMPLIMENTS

I've been fishing for Compliments
   with baited breath
      in the river of life.
So far I've caught:
   a "My, what a clever boy,"
     a "Hi, handsome,"
       a "What a man," and
         a "You're really funny."

I did catch a Small Insult
   but I threw it back.

MISS MELANIE MISH

Here is a picture of Melanie Mish

She hails from the planet of Flong.

She weighs 14 tons and she smells of old fish.

If you think that she's ugly—you're wrong!

For before you, you see the most beautiful Flonger

The planet of Flong's ever seen.

If you think that she's ugly, you couldn't be wronger.

Meet Melanie Mish—BEAUTY QUEEN!

I JUST DON'T BELIEVE
IN AEROPLANES

I've flown round this world of ours several times.
I've gobbled the food and I've guzzled the wines.
I've sat watching cabin staff doing their mimes
But I just don't believe in aeroplanes.

I've had it explained to me time and again,
Aeronautical experts have all tried in vain,
But I can't take it in 'cause the whole thing's insane!
I just don't believe in aeroplanes.

"It's simple," they say, to persuade me to shift,
"The action of airflow on wings causes lift."
It's round about then that my mind comes adrift!
I just don't believe in aeroplanes.

What pushes me over the brink of despair
Is you fly through the clouds on a wing and a prayer,
Supported by nothing but six miles of—AIR!
I just don't believe in aeroplanes.

Here's what we're looking at, here is the deal:
That four hundred tons of plastic and steel
Can float through the air, well excuse me—get real!
I just don't believe in aeroplanes.

UNDER A CLOUD

The sun is shining everywhere
    Except above my head.
I think the best thing I could do
    Is spend the day in bed.

SUMMER IS THE SILLY SEASON

Summer is the silly season,
    Everyone goes mad.
Everyone takes off their clothes,
    Even Mom and Dad!

ARE WE NEARLY THERE YET?

To be read in a monotonous drone of a voice. Start reciting this poem right at the beginning of a journey and just carry on and on and on and on and on . . . . Please adapt to suit circumstances: "Daddy are we there yet?" etc.

Mommy are we there yet,

Are we nearly there?

Mommy are we there yet,

Are we nearly there?

Mommy are we there yet,

Are we nearly there?

Mommy are we there yet,

Are we nearly there?

Mommy are we there yet,

Are we nearly there?

Mommy are we there yet,

Are we nearly there?

Mommy are we there yet,

Are we nearly there?

Mommy are we there yet,

Are we nearly there?

Mommy are we there yet,

Are we nearly there?
Mommy are we there yet,
Are we nearly there?
Mommy are we there yet,
Are we nearly there?
Mommy are we there yet,
Are we nearly there?
Mommy are we there yet,
Are we nearly there?
Mommy are we there yet,
Are we nearly there?
Mommy are we there yet,
Are we nearly there?
Mommy are we there yet,
Are we nearly there?
Mommy are we there yet,
Are we nearly there?
Mommy are we there yet,
Are we nearly there?
Mommy are we there yet,
Are we nearly there?
Mommy are we there yet,
Are we nearly there?
Mommy are we there yet,
Are we nearly there?
Mommy are we there yet,
Are we nearly there?
Mommy are we there yet,
Are we nearly there?
Mommy are we there yet,
Are we nearly there?
Mommy are we we there yet,
Are we nearly there?
Mommy are we we there yet,
Are we nearly there?
Mommy are we we there yet,
Are we nearly there?
Mommy are we we there yet,
Are we nearly there?

WARNING TO THOSE PERSONS THINKING OF TAKING A TRIP TO THE MOUNTAIN-OUS REGIONS THIS WINTER, PULLING ON A PAIR OF BOOTS THAT MAKE YOU WALK LIKE FRANKENSTEIN'S MONSTER, PUTTING ON FIFTEEN LAYERS OF CLOTHING TOPPED BY A MULTI-COLORED ROMPER, GOING SO HIGH UP A MOUNTAIN YOU CAN HARDLY BREATHE, STRAPPING TWO HUGE PLANKS TO YOUR FEET AND PUSHING YOURSELF OFF THE TOP:

Slush in the mush,
Slush in the mush.
You'll just end up with
Slush in the mush.

GETTING CARRIED AWAY

I was sitting out back in my rocking chair,
Just passing the time of day.
When a terrible wind done picked me up
And I got carried away.

It carried me over the mountains
And dropped me in the bay.
A humpback whale came sailing by
And I got carried away.

It carried me over the ocean
With its billowy salty spray.
It flipped me into the eye of a storm
And I got carried away.

The storm blew high and mighty,
A swirl of leaden gray.
It dumped me into the back of a truck
And I got carried away.

That truck went over the prairies
Where the dear old anchovies play.
It flicked me onto the back of a horse
And I got carried away.

Well, I rode home and told my mom
Where I had been all day.
She shook her head and then she said:
"Oh, you do get carried away,
Sometimes,
You do get carried away."

I FEEL SICK!

Set off before dawn, sick,
    Feeling very, yawn, sick,
Wish I'd not been born, sick,
    I FEEL SICK!

Is it very far, sick,
    Ate a chocolate bar, sick,
Feeling very carsick,
    I FEEL SICK!

Corner of my eye, sick,
    Trees are flashing by, sick,
Wish that I could die, sick,
    I FEEL SICK!

Dad says "look ahead," sick,
    Wish that I was dead, sick,
Take me home to bed, sick,
    I FEEL SICK!

Queasy, woozy, hot, sick,
    My brother says I'm not sick,
Thanks a rotten lot, sick,
    I FEEL SICK!

Twisty, turny road, sick,
    Chocolate overload, sick,
Ready to explode, sick,
    I FEEL SICK!

Daddy, hurry up, sick,
    Feel it coming up, sick,
Hic! Hiccup! Hiccup! Sick!
    I'VE BEEN SICK!

P.S.

Didn't make the door, sick.
    Threw up on the floor, sick.
There isn't any more sick.

I FEEL FINE!

LEMMY WAS A PILOT

Lemmy was a pilot,
A topnotch pilot,
Lemmy was a pilot,
Six years old.

Lemmy flew around the world,
All the way around the world,
Single-handed round the world,
Go, Lemmy, go!

Lemmy in the pilot's seat
Didn't stop to drink or eat,
Had a record time to beat,
Go, Lemmy, go!

Beat the record easily
But boy did Lemmy need to pee
(It rained that night on Tennessee),
Go, Lemmy, go!

And at the height of Lemmy's fame,
Lemmy quit the flying game—
Lemmy found it much too tame,
Go, Lemmy, go!

Now Lemmy is an astronaut,
An outer-space-type astronaut,
The fly-across-the-cosmos sort.
Go, Lemmy, go!

THE TEACHER'S HOLIDAY LAMENT

Good-bye blue skies,
  Hello rain.
Just got back
  From a month in Spain.

Good-bye new friends
  Left behind.
Hello back to
  Daily grind.

Good-bye hotel
  Swimming pool.
Good-bye beaches,
  Hello school.

Hello puddles,
  Good-bye sea.
Hello gray skies,
  Poor old me.

Hello clouds,
  Good-bye sun.
Hello school,
  Good-bye fun.

Good-bye hours
  Of peace and quiet.
Hello daily
  Classroom riot.

(Yes, I know this poem goes on a bit, but then, so do some teachers I know.)

SEA SAW ME

When I was three I went to see
  The sea and let the sea see me.
    Sea see me see me see sea.
      I saw the sea and the sea saw me.

AAAAHHHRREEAAAHHREEEAAA—OUCH!

Tarzan's recovering,
  Coming on fine.
We're close to discovering
  Who greased the vine.

FOOT SLOGGING

Our teacher, striding out in front,
Shouts: "Walking's good for us!"
The kids, as one, all answer back:

WE'D RATHER TAKE THE BUS!

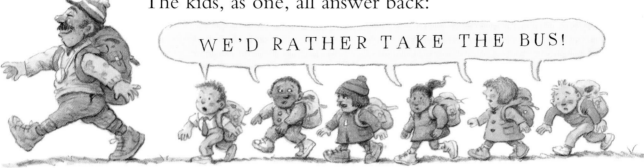

A FLIGHT OF FANCY

I planted a packet of birdseed
In a line as straight as an arrow.
I didn't get much in the way of a crop,
Just a parrot, two ducks, and a sparrow.

STROLLIN'
DOWN THE HIGHWAY
LEAVIN' HOME TRAVELIN' BLUES

Well, I'm strollin' down the highway
    With my suitcase in my hand.
Said I'm strollin' down the highway,
    I've got my suitcase in my hand.
You know I left my home this mornin'—
    Gonna travel 'cross this land.

Well, I'm strollin' down the highway,
    You know I've left my mom and dad.
Said I'm strollin' down the highway,
    You know I've left my mom an' dad.
When they find I'm missin'—
    Boy, will they be mad.

Yeah, I'm strollin' down the highway,
    An' the rain is in my shoes.
Strollin' down the highway,
    Rain is sloppin' in my shoes.
You know I'm feelin' mighty lonesome—
    Yeah, I've got those travelin' blues.

Strollin' down the highway,
    Got my teddy by my side.
Strollin' down the highway,
    Got my teddy by my side.
I ain't never goin' home again—
    You know a fella's got his pride.

I'm strollin' down the highway
    When a car begins to slow.
Said I'm strollin' down the highway,
    When a car begins to slow.
This guy looks down an' smiles at me—
    Says, "Where you wanna go?"

Well, I'm ridin' down the highway,
    My strollin' days are done.
Yeah, I'm ridin' down the highway,
    Yeah, my strollin' days are done.
My mommy's in the back seat—
    Sayin', "We sure missed you, son."

I'm *ridin'* down the highway
    An' I've lost the urge to roam.
Yes, I'm *ridin'* down the highway,
    An' I've lost that urge to roam.
I look up at the driver . . .
    An' say, "Daddy, take me home."

IT'S A SMALL WORLD

(The first paragraph from my forthcoming science-fiction novel.)

"It's a small world," said the Mega-Ultimate-Space-Beast as he potted the Earth into a black hole; making it six straight wins.

The Mega-Ultimate-Space-Beast Universal Galaxy Pool All-Comers Championship was his. Okay, so it was a crummy little competition, held in a stinking backwater, but he was young, and who knew what the future held in store . . .

FRANKENSTEIN'S MONSTER WORLD TOUR

I left my heart in San Francisco,
My torso in Nepal,
My arms in Valparaiso
And my legs in Montreal.

I lost my ears in New York City
And in Trinidad, my hair.
Lost my memory in . . .
(Now where was it I lost my memory?)
Oh, I can't remember where.

And if that wasn't bad enough
I think I'm losing my voice . . .

48

DAZE OF THE WEEK

On Sunday we saw Paris,
On Monday, Amsterdam.
Tuesday—Barcelona,
Wednesday, Siam.

Thursday was Australia.
Friday we saw Rome.
Saturday was Africa
And then we all came home.

A ROVING EYE

I have a roving eye.
It swivels round and round.
And when I'm looking at the stars
It's staring at the ground.

I have a roving eye.
No choice in where it goes.
I'll try to look you in the eye
But might look up your nose.

A-roving, a-roving,
I have a roving eye.
It swivels right, it swivels left,
I have a roving eye.

I have a roving eye.
I've no control at all.
It simply won't behave itself,
It drives me up the wall.

49

THE SQUIDGEREE

Way down deep
At the bottom of the sea
Lives a marvelous fish
Called the Squidgeree.

It's got no bones
And it's got no skin.
It's got no tail
And it's got no fin.

It's got no mouth
And it's got no eyes.
It tells no secrets,
Tells no lies.

It doesn't eat
And it doesn't swim.
No luminous light,
So it's very dim.

If you approach
With stealth and care,
You'll find the Squidgeree's
Not there.

It's a marvelous fish,
The Squidgeree.
The most marvelous fish
You'll never see.

LIGHT NIGHTS, NIGHT LIGHTS

I think the Sun should be shining at night.
It's *then* that the world and its people need light,
Rather than during the day when we don't.
I'm sure you'll agree, but then maybe you won't.

TIME WARPED

With the wonders of modern technology
And the latest in warp-factor flight,
If you leave home on Saturday morning,
You can get home the previous night.

ALIENS ON VACATION

They come from planets near and far,
Some big, some small, some quite bizarre.
Twinkle, twinkle, little star—
Aliens on vacation!

They've read the brochures, booked hotels,
Had their shots and said farewells.
Run for cover! Ring them bells!
Aliens on vacation!

Toward the Earth the pilot steers.
They've come to look for souvenirs,
Eat some pizza, drink some beers—
Aliens on vacation!

If you stare, they'll start a fight.
They sing rude songs and dance all night.
They go to bed when it gets light—
Aliens on vacation!

They hog the lounge chairs round the pool,
Splash other guests and play the fool.
They write with spray paint ALIENS RULE!
Aliens on vacation!

They plunder, photograph, and scour.
Their spaceship has enormous power.
It takes on board the Eiffel Tower . . .
Aliens on vacation!

From Israel, the Wailing Wall!
From London Town, the Albert Hall!
They take Mount Everest from Nepal . . .
Aliens on vacation!

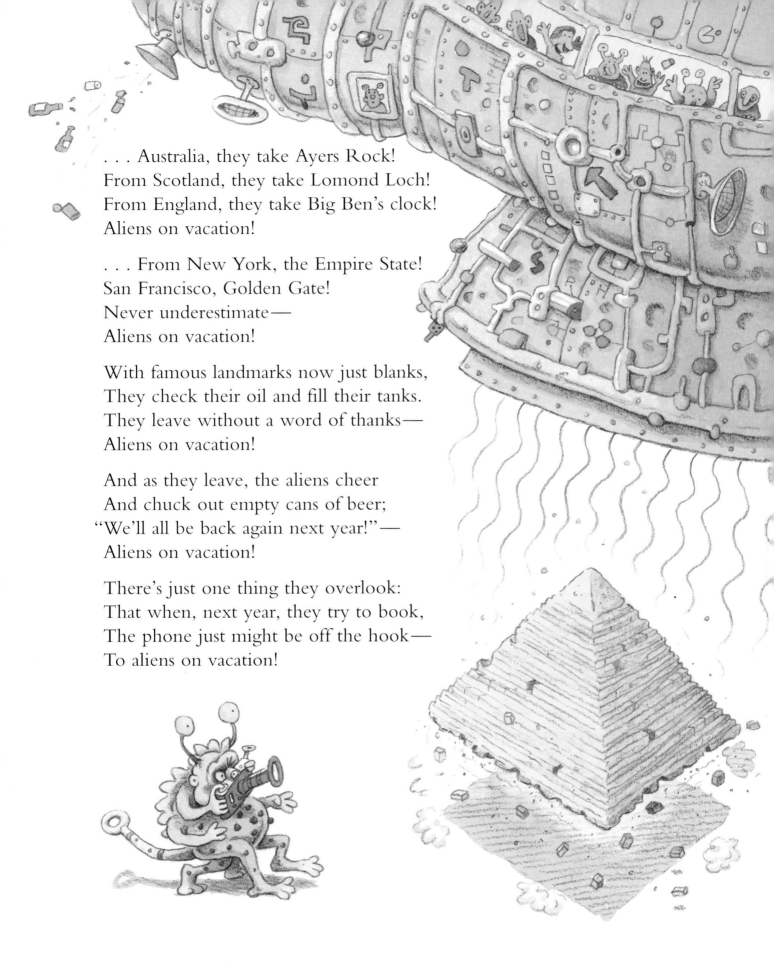

. . . Australia, they take Ayers Rock!
From Scotland, they take Lomond Loch!
From England, they take Big Ben's clock!
Aliens on vacation!

. . . From New York, the Empire State!
San Francisco, Golden Gate!
Never underestimate—
Aliens on vacation!

With famous landmarks now just blanks,
They check their oil and fill their tanks.
They leave without a word of thanks—
Aliens on vacation!

And as they leave, the aliens cheer
And chuck out empty cans of beer;
"We'll all be back again next year!"—
Aliens on vacation!

There's just one thing they overlook:
That when, next year, they try to book,
The phone just might be off the hook—
To aliens on vacation!

THAT FUNNY FEELING YOU GET
IN RAILWAY TUNNELS

As the train went through the railway tunnel,
the little girl looked up at her mommy and said:
"I've gone all quiet and my voice
has gone funny."
And I knew just what she meant.

DOWN IN THE DUMPS

I'm down in the dumps
On vacation.
Surrounded by garbage,
That's me.
Some people might say
That it's rubbish.
But it's great
'Cause I'm broke
And it's free!

PANIC ON TITANIC

I was riding a ship of the desert,
    Its name it was Titanic,
I should have been suspicious,
    But I'm not a man to panic.

I was riding a ship of the desert,
    When I heard a terrible clunk!
I'd run into a sandberg
    And my ship of the desert sunk.

AS I WENT WALKING

As I went walking out one day
I met a man and he did say:
"Fiddle-dee-rollop, fiddle-dee-ree
Rumpety-ti-doe, rumpety-dee."

As I went walking the following day
I met a fair maid and she did say:
"Whimple, whample, wobble-bum-ho.
Swample, fwample, stickle-back-po."

As I went walking the very next day
I met an old lady and she did say:
"Hubble-dee, bubble-dee, stinky-poo,
Yankee-doodle, toodle-oo."

As I went walking on the fourth day
I met a small child and she did say:
"Have you noticed there are some
really weird people around here?"

On the fifth day I stayed home.

A SHORT OLD SAILING POEM

I set off in my sailing boat;
I wore my brand new overcoat.
And had that boat been stronger,
My poem would have been longer.

(And had that coat been lighter,
My future, somewhat brighter.)

GOING NOWHERE, FAST

I'm going slightly round the twist,

I'm going round the bend.

I'm going round in circles.

I've fallen down. The end.

AAAAHHHRREEAAAHHREEEAAA
—Ouch! / **42**

A Flight of Fancy / **43**

Aliens on Vacation / **52**

All I Ask Is a Perfect Day / **20**

Are We Nearly There Yet? / **34**

A Roving Eye / **49**

A Sad Case / **21**

A Short Old Sailing Poem / **57**

As I Went Walking / **56**

A Sting in the Tail / **18**

Counting on You (A Love Letter) / **22**

Daze of the Week / **49**

Down in the Dumps / **55**

First Draft of the Most Famous
Australian Song Ever / **24**

Fishing for Compliments / **29**

Foot Slogging / **43**

Frankenstein's Monster World Tour / **48**

Getting Carried Away / **37**

Going Nowhere, Fast / **58**

I Feel Sick! / **38**

If I Could Fly Like Icarus / **17**

If You're Traveling in Transylvania / **23**

I Just Don't Believe in
Aeroplanes / **32**

I'm Off to Treasure Island / **12**

It's a Small World / **46**

Lemmy Was a Pilot / **40**

Light Nights, Night Lights / **51**

Miss Melanie Mish / **30**

No Room to Swing a Cat! / **28**

Panic on Titanic / 55

Row, Row, Row Your Bath / 21

Sea Saw Me / 42
Strollin' Down the
   Highway Leavin' Home
   Travelin' Blues / 44
Summer Is the Silly Season / 33

That Funny Feeling You Get in
   Railway Tunnels / 54
The Armchair Traveler / 15
The Nomad Rush / 16
The Oozily Woozily Plonk / 10
The Postcard / 15
The Squidgeree / 50
The Teacher's Holiday Lament / 41
Time Warped / 51

Under a Cloud / 33

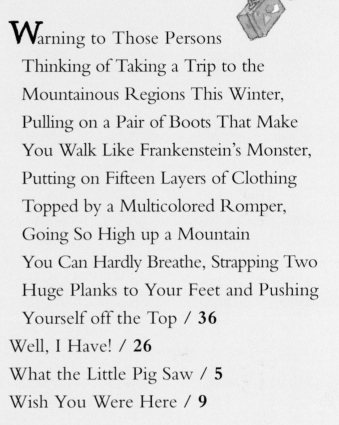

Warning to Those Persons
Thinking of Taking a Trip to the
Mountainous Regions This Winter,
Pulling on a Pair of Boots That Make
You Walk Like Frankenstein's Monster,
Putting on Fifteen Layers of Clothing
Topped by a Multicolored Romper,
Going So High up a Mountain
You Can Hardly Breathe, Strapping Two
Huge Planks to Your Feet and Pushing
Yourself off the Top / 36
Well, I Have! / 26
What the Little Pig Saw / 5
Wish You Were Here / 9

Yet Another Poem to Send to Your
Worst Enemy / 14